D1010905

Digger and Daisy

Plant a Garden

By Judy Young
Illustrated by Dana Sullivan

Look for other books in the Digger and Daisy series

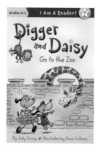   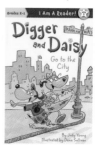

This book has a reading comprehension level of 1.8 under the ATOS® readability formula.
For information about ATOS please visit www.renlearn.com.
ATOS is a registered trademark of Renaissance Learning, Inc.

Lexile®, Lexile® Framework and the Lexile® logo are trademarks of MetaMetrics, Inc.,
and are registered in the United States and abroad. The trademarks and names of other
companies and products mentioned herein are the property of their respective owners.
Copyright © 2010 MetaMetrics, Inc. All rights reserved.

Sleeping Bear Press™

2395 South Huron Parkway, Suite 200
Ann Arbor, MI 48104
www.sleepingbearpress.com

Printed and bound in the United States.

10 9 8 7 6 5 4 3 2 1 (case)
10 9 8 7 6 5 4 3 2 1 (pbk)

Library of Congress Cataloging-in-Publication Data

Names: Young, Judy, author. | Sullivan, Dana, illustrator.
Title: Digger and Daisy plant a garden / written by Judy Young;
illustrated by Dana Sullivan.
Description: Ann Arbor, MI : Sleeping Bear Press, [2016] | Series: Digger and Daisy; book 6 |
Summary: Daisy suggests to her brother, Digger, that they plant a garden so Digger digs the holes and
Daisy plants seeds for carrots, tomatoes, and other vegetables, while Digger plants a tasty surprise.
Identifiers: LCCN 2015027641| ISBN 9781585369317 (hard cover : alk. paper) |
ISBN 9781585369324 (paperback : alk. paper)
Subjects: | CYAC: Gardening—Fiction. | Brothers and sisters—Fiction. | Dogs—Fiction.
Classification: LCC PZ7.Y8664 Dil 2016 | DDC [E]—dc23
LC record available at http://lccn.loc.gov/2015027641

For Elia, Leif, and Cash Hurtado
—Judy

To that little sprout, Amie.
—Dana

It is spring.

"Let's plant a garden," says Daisy.

"We will grow good things to eat."

Digger digs holes.

Daisy puts in seeds.

Digger covers them with dirt.

"Carrots will grow here,"
says Daisy.
"Carrots are good to eat."

Digger digs more holes.

Daisy puts in more seeds.

Digger covers them with dirt.

"This will be lettuce," says Daisy.

"That will be tomatoes.

And peppers will grow there.

They are good to eat."

Daisy waters the garden.

But Digger digs another hole.

He puts something in it.

He does not let Daisy see.

"What are you planting?"

says Daisy.

"A surprise," says Digger.

"You will see."

"Is it good to eat?" says Daisy.

"Yes," says Digger.

"It is good to eat."

Digger and Daisy go to the
garden every day.

One day they see something.

"Look," says Digger.

"There are leaves."

Daisy looks.

Then she looks at the last spot.

"Nothing is growing," says Daisy.

"There is only dirt.

What did you plant?"

"A surprise," says Digger.

"It will be good to eat."

More days go by.

"Look," says Digger.

"Now the plants are tall."

Daisy looks.

Then she looks at the last spot.

"Nothing is growing," says Daisy.

"There is only dirt.

What did you plant?"

"A surprise," says Digger.

"You will see.

It will be good to eat."

More days go by.

"Look," says Digger.

"There are yellow flowers."

"Yes," says Daisy.

"They will turn into tomatoes.

Tomatoes are good to eat."

"And look here," says Digger.

"There are white flowers too."

"Yes," says Daisy.

"Those will turn into peppers.

Peppers are good to eat too."

Daisy looks at the last spot.

"Nothing is growing,"

says Daisy.

"There is only dirt.

What did you plant?"

"You will see," says Digger.

"It is a surprise.

But it will be good to eat."

Many days go by.

The peppers grow big.

The tomatoes turn red.

"The garden is ready,"

says Daisy.

"We have many good things
to eat. Pull on this plant."
Digger pulls.
Up comes a carrot.

"I will cut some lettuce," says
Daisy.

"You can pick peppers.
Pick tomatoes too."

"We made a good garden,"
says Digger.

"Yes," says Daisy.

"Now let's eat."

"Wait," says Digger.

"There is one more thing."

Digger looks at the last spot.

Daisy looks too.

"Nothing is growing," says Daisy.

"There is only dirt.

What did you plant?"

"A surprise," says Digger.

"Dig it up."

Daisy digs in the dirt.

She pulls something out.

"A bone?" says Daisy.

"You planted a bone?"

"Yes," says Digger.

"And it will be good to eat!"